For Adele and Samuel
~ IG

For Rebecca
~ TW

This edition copyright © 2001
Baby's First Book Club®
Bristol, PA 19007
Originally published in Great Britain 2001
by Little Tiger Press, London
an imprint of Magi Publications
Text © 2001 Isobel Gamble
Illustrations © 2001 Tim Warnes
Printed in China
ISBN 1-58048-196-5

Isobel Gamble and Tim Warnes

Who's That?

BARRON'S

Daisy Dog was tired.
She made her way to
her cozy kennel for
an afternoon snooze.
But . . .

"Who's that sleeping
in my kennel?" she
yawned.

Snorter trotted and snorted all the way home, only to discover that someone got there before him.

"Who's that dozing in my sty?" he oinked.

"It's Dabble Duck!
This is *my* sty, Dabble.
It's for pigs, not ducks."

Feeling very tired,
Dabble swam across
the pond to her nest.
But two long fluffy
brown ears were
poking up from
behind the rushes.

"Who's that snoozing
in my nest?" quacked
Dabble.

Racer skipped and hopped across the meadow, but he spotted a bushy tail sticking out of his cozy burrow. *Someone* was there already.

"Who's that snoring in my burrow?" he twitched.

Sandy scrambled off up
a tree, looking forward
to a long deep sleep.
She noticed two tiny
pink ears popping up
between the leaves.

"Who's that snoozing
and snoring in my
hole?" she sniffed.

Merry scuttled back to her own little mousehole, only to discover someone *very* big and *very* furry lying right across it.

"I know who th-that is," she squeaked.

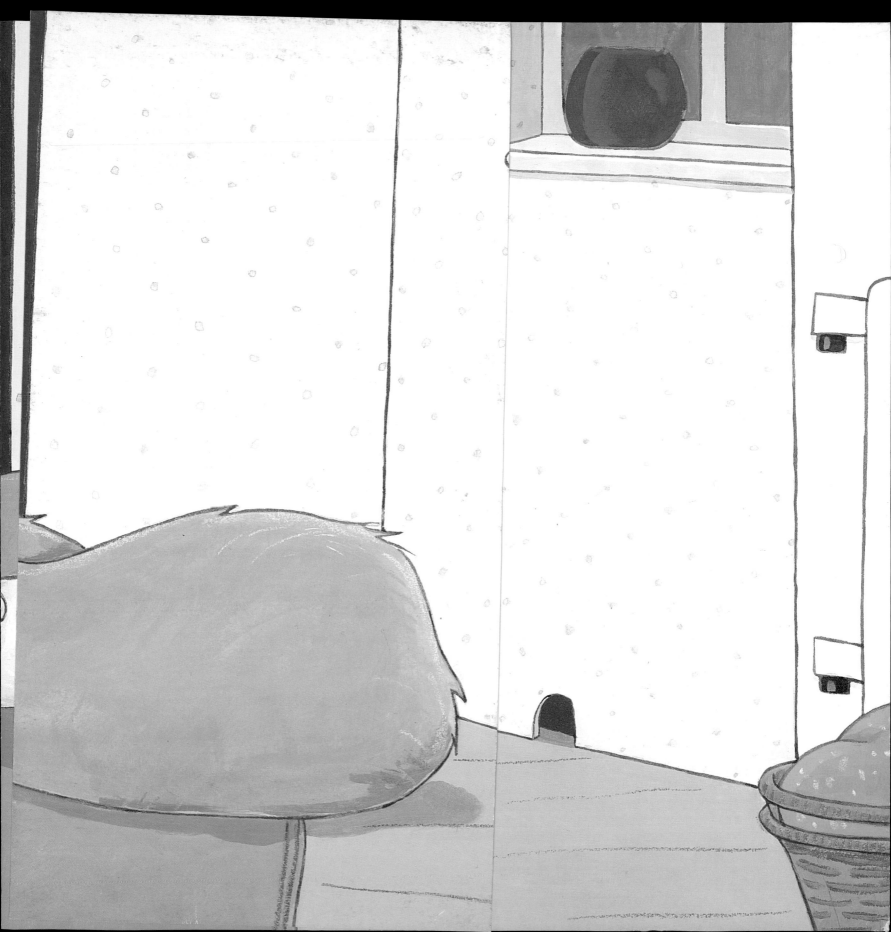

It was Merry's lucky day. Caspar was far too tired to catch mice. He slowly got up and made his way to his very own bed. But someone cute and cuddly was already sleeping there.

"Who's that sleeping beneath my favorite blanket?" he meowed.

"It's Poppy Puppy!
This is *my* basket.
You should be snuggled
up in your own bed."

Poppy padded wearily home. It was getting late and she was very tired. But . . .

"Who's that cuddled up in my kennel?" she yelped.

"So
sm
pas
to s